Chapter 1

Catch That Jynx!

"What kind of Pokémon is that?" Ash Ketchum asked.

Like every Pokémon trainer, Ash was always on the lookout for new Pokémon. Today, he spotted one on a sunny beach. His friends Brock and Misty sat next to him on the sand. Pikachu, his Electric

Pokémon, was by his side.

The new Pokémon stood by the waves. It had long yellow hair, and it wore a red dress.

Ash took out Dexter, his small computer. Dexter held facts about every kind of Pokémon.

"Jynx, the human shape Pokémon," said Dexter. "This Pokémon can put other Pokémon to sleep with its Lovely Kiss."

Holiday Hi-Jynx

A Pokémon Sticker Storybook

Adapted by Tracey West

SCHOLASTIC INC.

New York   Toronto   London   Auckland   Sydney

Mexico City   New Delhi   Hong Kong   Buenos Aires

ISBN 0-439-31750-9

12 11 10 9 8 7 6 5 4 3 2 1   1 2 3 4 5 6/0

Printed in the U.S.A.
First Scholastic printing, November 2001

"I have got to catch that Pokémon!" Ash said.

He turned to Pikachu. "Use Thundershock," Ash said.

The little yellow Pokémon jumped into the air. Pikachu sizzled Jynx with an electric shock.

Jynx picked up Pikachu. It gave Pikachu a big Kiss! Pikachu's eyes closed. The little Pokémon fell asleep.

"Jynx used the Lovely Kiss Attack," said Misty.

Ash took out a Poké Ball. "I am not done yet!" Ash threw the ball.

A small orange Pokémon popped out of the ball.

It was

Flames came out of Charmander's mouth. The flames hit Jynx. The Pokémon looked frazzled.

Now Jynx was weak. Ash might be able to catch it. Ash took out another Poké Ball. He started to throw it at Jynx.

"Wait, Ash!" Misty cried. "That is no ordinary Jynx!"

Chapter 2
Santa Jynx

"What do you mean, Misty?" asked Ash.

Misty pointed to Jynx. The Pokémon held a black boot in its hand.

"It might belong to another trainer," said Misty. "A wild Jynx would not be holding a boot."

Misty smiled at the Jynx, and Jynx handed her the boot. Misty looked inside.

A picture of Santa Claus was stamped inside the boot!

Misty showed everyone the picture.

"Pika!" Pikachu was excited to see Santa's face.

"Maybe Santa Claus is Jynx's trainer," said Brock.

"Jynx! Jynx!" said Jynx.

Strands of Jynx's long hair reached out and touched Ash and the others on the forehead. Then Jynx used its psychic power. It put a story into their minds.

In his mind, Ash saw a snowy

place. Jynx was sitting on an ice-berg. It was shining Santa's boot.

Then the iceberg cracked and floated away. Jynx drifted across the sea. Then it landed on the beach, far from home.

"What a sad story," said Misty.

"This is terrible," said Brock. "Santa Claus needs his Jynx. And his boot! He cannot deliver pre-sents without them."

Ash looked across the ocean.

"There is only one thing to do," Ash said. "We will take Jynx back to the North Pole!"

Chapter 3

Long Trip

Ash and his friends found a raft.
They set sail across the sea.

They sailed and sailed. But the
raft did not move very fast.

"I have an idea," Misty told Ash.

Misty threw out four Poké Balls.
Starmie, Staryu, and Goldeen
splashed into the water, but

Psyduck stayed on the raft. The orange duck Pokémon did not like the water.

Ash threw a Poké Ball, too. Out popped a cute Pokémon with a hard shell. It was

Squirtle jumped into the sea. Ash and Misty tied ropes around the Water Pokémon. The Pokémon swam fast. They pulled the raft behind them.

The Water Pokémon began to get very tired.

"I will help!" said Ash. He tied a rope around his ankle and jumped into the water.

The Water Pokémon climbed onto the raft. While they rested, Ash pulled the raft.

Soon Ash got tired, too.

"We will never get to the North Pole," Ash said. Then Ash heard a strange voice.

"You are almost there. Keep going."

"Did you hear that?" Ash asked

Misty and Brock.

"We did not hear anything," Misty said. Then Misty's eyes grew wide. "Ash, look out!"

A giant wave was rising up in front of them. The wave crashed over the boat. It pushed Ash deep into the water.

Ash opened his eyes. He had to swim to the top!

Then Ash stopped. Something was swimming toward him.

Something very big!

Chapter 4
Lapras

A big blue Pokémon swam toward him. It was a

It had four strong flippers. It scooped Ash up on its back. Then it swam to the top.

Ash gasped for air. The Pokémon had saved him!

"Who are you?" Ash asked it.

"I am Lapras," said a voice in Ash's head. But the Pokémon's mouth did not move.

"Are you speaking into my mind?" Ash asked.

Lapras nodded.

Misty reached for Dexter.

"Lapras is a smart Pokémon," said Dexter. "It can understand human speech. Lapras likes to carry humans on its back."

"*Santa sent me to find Jynx,*" said Lapras.

Misty and Brock looked surprised. They had heard its voice, too.

"*You were very kind to help Jynx,*" said Lapras. "*Now I will help you get to Santa's workshop.*"

"Yay!" said Misty.

Misty and Brock tied the ropes to Lapras. Lapras pulled the raft across the sea. Ash rode on Lapras's back.

Soon it began to get very cold. The friends shivered. Ash climbed back onto the raft. Jynx wrapped Ash, Misty, Brock, and Pikachu in its long hair. It was the only way to stay warm.

"We are almost there," Lapras said.

Ash was freezing. He hoped Lapras was right.

Then the shore came in sight.

Giant ice crystals formed a shimmering wall.

"That is where Santa lives," said Lapras.

"Finally!" Ash said.

But something was wrong. The sea began to churn, and a giant submarine rose out of the water. The sub looked like a Gyarados, a blue Pokémon with a scary face.

"Prepare for trouble!" someone yelled.

Chapter 5

Santa's Workshop

A door opened on top of the Gyarados submarine. A boy and girl climbed out.

Ash knew them. They were Jessie and James from Team Rocket! The Pokémon thieves were always getting in his way. What were they up to now?

"We were going to set a trap for Santa," said Jessie. "But this is better. You have led us right to him."

"Now let us have him!" said James.

"Have who?" Ash asked.

"Santa," said Jessie. She pointed to Jynx. "He is right there on that raft."

"That is not Santa," said Ash. "That is a Jynx."

"You cannot fool me," said Jessie. "I know that Santa is really a Jynx! When I was a little girl, a Jynx came into my room on

Christmas Eve. That Jynx was dressed just like Santa Claus!"

Jessie and James jumped down. They landed on the raft.

Then a Pokémon popped out of the sub. It was

Meowth shot a long tube into the sky. Two nets flew out of the tube. Jessie and James grabbed Jynx. They jumped off of the raft just as one net covered Ash and his friends. Another net covered Lapras. Team Rocket had trapped them all!

Jessie, James, and Meowth ran away. They carried the captured Jynx.

"What are we going to do now?" asked Meowth.

"We will get revenge," said Jessie. "The night that Jynx came on Christmas Eve, it stole my favorite doll! Then it left and did not come back. I did not get any toys."

Jessie pointed to the gate made of ice crystals. "Now we will raid Santa's workshop. We will steal every toy there! We will teach this Santa Jynx a lesson."

Team Rocket ran through the gate. Santa's workshop looked like a big Christmas tree made of ice.

Jessie looked in the window.

Jynx filled the workshop. They were all making toys.

"This is strange," Jessie said. "I did not know there were so many Santas."

"Look!" James said. He pointed into the workshop.

A chubby man was putting toys into a bag. He wore a red suit and one black boot. He had a white beard.

"It is the real Santa Claus!" said Meowth.

"Maybe I was wrong," said Jessie. "Maybe Jynx is not Santa Claus."

"We can still steal all these presents!" said Meowth.

"Right!" said Jessie. Team Rocket burst into the workshop.

"I miss my Jynx," Santa Claus

was saying. "And I sure could use my other boot."

"Is this what you are looking for?" Jessie asked. She held out Santa's boot.

Just then, Ash, Misty, Brock, and Pikachu ran in.

"Watch out, Santa," said Ash, "those three are on your naughty list!"

"What is going on?" Santa asked.

James and Meowth tied up Santa with a strong rope.

"It looks like you will be tied up

this Christmas," James joked.

Ash and his friends tried to stop Team Rocket. But James and Meowth tied them up, too.

Then Team Rocket brought everyone outside. Jessie made the Jynx take all the toys out of the workshop. She made them pile the toys into the submarine.

"Why are you doing this?" asked Santa.

"Quiet!" said Jessie. "I am making up for the presents I never got."

Santa looked confused. "What do you mean?" he asked.

"When I was a little girl, a Jynx came into my room on Christmas Eve," said Jessie. "It stole my favorite doll. And I never got another present from Santa again."

Then Jessie felt a tap on her shoulder. It was

Jynx held a wooden doll.

"My doll!" said Jessie

"Jynx knocked over your doll and it broke," said Santa. "Then Jynx brought the doll to me so I could fix it. But you thought Jynx stole it. You did not believe in me anymore. I can only give presents to people who believe in me."

Jessie had tears in her eyes. "I am sorry, Jynx," Jessie said. She hugged the Pokémon. "Please forgive me."

"Does this mean you will give back the presents?" Santa asked.

Jessie smiled an evil smile. "Ha!" she said. "I am not *that* sorry. These presents belong to us!"

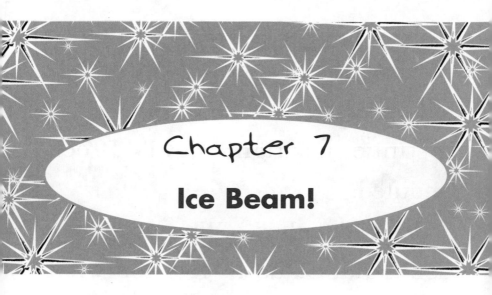

Chapter 7

Ice Beam!

"See you later!" Jessie cried. She jumped on top of the submarine. James and Meowth jumped on next.

The Gyarados sub started to sail away.

Ash tried to get out of the ropes. But they were too tight.

"Come back here!" he called out.

"Give back those presents!" yelled Misty.

"Untie us right now!" Brock shouted.

Jessie laughed. "Why don't you ask Santa Claus to give you what you want?" she said.

Team Rocket climbed into the sub.

"It looks like Team Rocket has stolen Christmas!" Misty wailed.

"Not yet," said Ash. "Look!"

Lapras swam toward the submarine. It shot a freezing beam of

ice out of its mouth.

The ice beam froze the subma-rine. It could not move.

Then Ash wriggled one hand free and threw a Poké Ball. Charmander popped out. The orange Pokémon used its fire power to burn through the ropes and set Ash free.

Ash jumped to his feet. "Let's stop Team Rocket and save Christmas. Use Fire Spin Attack!"

Charmander blasted the submarine with a spinning flame. Jessie, James, and Meowth came flying out.

"Thanks for the defrost!" laughed Meowth.

James threw a Poké Ball. A purple Pokémon with two heads floated out. It was

"Weezing, Sludge Attack!" James yelled.

Black goo poured out of Weezing's mouth. The sludge hit Charmander in the face.

Team Rocket jumped back into the submarine.

"You will not stop us this time!" James said.

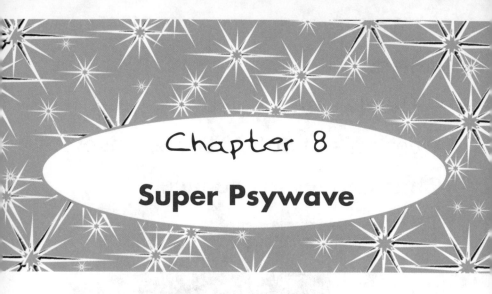

Chapter 8

Super Psywave

"They are getting away again!" Ash cried.

He turned to Santa Claus. "I am sorry," he said.

Santa smiled. "Do not worry. We will get them back." Santa turned to his Jynx helpers. "All right," he said. "Use your Psywave!"

All of the Jynx stood on the icy shore. They began to make a strange sound. *"Jyyyyyyynx! Jyyyyyyynx!"*

Inside the submarine, Team Rocket was pedaling fast. They were trying to get the sub away from the North Pole.

But the strange music of the Jynx surrounded them. They felt weird.

"Our feet are moving, but we are not going anywhere!" said Meowth.

Onshore, Ash watched as the submarine floated out of the

water, like magic. The sub shook up and down in the air. The toys fell out of the sub's mouth.

The whole time, the Jynx kept up the Psywave. *"Jyyyyyynx! Jyyyyyyynx!"*

Soon all of the toys were back on the shore.

"I think we can say good-bye to the Psywave now," said Santa.

"Jyyyyyyyyyyyyyyyynx!" The Jynx sang one last, loud note.

Boom! The submarine exploded.

Team Rocket flew off into the sky.

41

"Looks like we are blasting off again!" they screamed.

Ash cheered. "We did it! We saved Christmas."

"Pikachu!" Pikachu was excited about something. It pointed into the sky.

Ash felt a cold snowflake on his nose.

"It's snowing!" Ash said happily.

Chapter 9
A Very Merry Christmas

The Jynx helped Santa load the toys onto his sleigh. Pikachu played in the falling

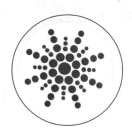

"It looks like we will have a white

Christmas," said Brock.

Ash slapped his forehead. "Oh, no!" he said. "I forgot to tell Santa what I want for Christmas. I guess I will not get a present this year."

Lapras swam up to the shore. The Pokémon smiled.

"*Santa knows,*" said Lapras.

The Jynx ran up to them. It held four presents in its arms. There was one each for Ash, Misty, Brock, and Pikachu.

"Thank you," Ash said.

Santa walked up to them.

"I have asked Lapras to take you

back where you came from," Santa said. "Thank you for your help. Now I must be on my way."

"Can we see your reindeer?" Misty asked.

Santa laughed. "Reindeer? I don't need reindeer." He pointed to his sleigh.

A Pokémon stood in front of the sleigh. Its long tail and mane were made of orange flames.
It was

Ash could not believe it. "This is one Christmas I will never forget," he said.

Pikachu smiled. *"Pika pika!"*